First published in Great Britain in 1987 by
George Weidenfeld and Nicolson Limited
91 Clapham High Street
London SW4 7TA

Origination by Imago Publishing Ltd
Printed and bound by LEGO, Vicenza, Italy

HAPPY CHRISTMAS, CLEM

by **BEATRICE PHILLPOTTS**
illustrated by **INGRAM PINN**

LAURA ASHLEY
WEIDENFELD AND NICOLSON
LONDON

It was snowing hard on the night of Clem's Christmas Adventure. Clem was excited. He was busy making plans for the next day.

'I could be a real snow hero,' thought Clem. 'I could save someone trapped in the snow. Or. . .'

'Time for bed, Clem,' said Dad.

And he switched off the light.

The next morning, the sun shone and the snow sparkled.
   Clem wanted to be taken for a walk.
   But Mum was busy making the Christmas pudding.
   'Do go away, Clem,' she said. 'You're putting
your paws in the butter.'

Perhaps Dad would help him build a snow dog.

But Dad was busy putting up the Christmas decorations. The stepladder rocked backwards and forwards.

'Get down, Clem,' he shouted, 'before you cause an accident!'

'Huh,' snorted Clem.
And he slunk away.

The snow felt cold and crunchy. Clem's paws made funny patterns in it.

Then Clem heard voices. Helen and Bertie were sledging on the hill.

'That looks like a good game,' thought Clem.

He raced up the hill to join them.

There were lots of people on the hill.
  Clem played 'Hunt the Snow Hare' with
Sally the Sheepdog. They had great fun charging
in and out of everyone's legs.
  'Watch where you're going, Clem,' warned Helen.
But it was too late. . .

Clem stepped back – onto Bertie's sledging tray. And he began to slide off down the hill. 'Jump off, Clem!' cried Sally. But Clem was too surprised to move. 'H-e-e-e-e-l-p,' he shouted, as he disappeared down the hill.

WOOMPH! Clem overbalanced
and fell flat on his back.
Still the tray whizzed on.

The hill was very steep.
Trees and sledgers flashed
by. Clem felt as if he was flying.
'I'm enjoying this,' he thought,
balancing on his back legs.

Clem overtook the vicar.

'I bet he's never seen a dog do this before,' thought Clem.

'Good Heavens,' exclaimed the vicar, as Clem rushed past.

Clem couldn't steer the tray. Instead of going
straight down the hill, it shot off to the right.
   Clem was heading straight for a fence!
A big sign on the fence said:
BEWARE OF THE BULL.
   'Oh no,' thought Clem.

BANG! The tray hit an enormous dark object. It was Bill the Bull.

Clem was catapulted up into the air. M-O-O-A-R-G-H, roared Bill.

W-H-E-E-E-E! Clem soared over the barn. Now he really was flying!

'Watch out, girls,' Clem shouted to the ducks and hens below.

THUMP! Down came Clem on the frozen pond.

SQUAWK! Up flew all the birds.

Even now Clem could not stop. It was like being on a skating rink.

The wind whistled through his fur. His claws made sparks on the ice. And on Clem slid.

The birds fluttered down again. They stood watching as Clem sailed past.

'Just call me Super Dog,' cried Clem.

'Mind the snow bank, Super Dog,' warned the birds.

Clem tried to stop but he was going too fast.
    'Well, at least the snow will be soft,' he thought.
    SPLAT! Clem hit the snow bank head on.
But even that did not stop him.
A moment later he was tumbling down
the other side towards the house.

Mum and Dad were
standing outside the house
by the Christmas tree. They
were listening to some carol singers.
Clem rolled faster and faster, gathering snow as he went.

'Make way for the Great White Snowball Dog,' he shouted. But his mouth was full of snow and no one heard him.

The next moment he found himself caught up in something very prickly. Clem had bounced into the Christmas tree!

Clem popped up out of the tree.
Everyone laughed – he looked so funny.
'Happy Christmas, Clem!' they cried.